A SIENA BOOK

Siena is an imprint of Parragon Books
Published by Parragon Book Service Ltd,
Units 13 - 17, Avonbridge Trading Estate,
Atlantic Road, Avonmouth, Bristol BS11 9QD

Original concept by Julian Tucki • Improved by Guy Parr
Developed by Caroline Repchuk and Dug Steer

Produced by The Templar Company plc,
Pippbrook Mill, London Road, Dorking, Surrey RH4 1JE

Copyright © 1996 Parragon Book Service Ltd

Edited by Caroline Repchuk
Designed by Janie Louise Hunt

Printed and bound in Italy

ISBN 0-75251-318-4

JIM JAM'S
Big Day Out

ILLUSTRATED BY STEPHANIE BOEY

WRITTEN BY CAROLINE REPCHUK

One fine spring morning the Jam Pandas were having breakfast together in the kitchen of Tumbledown Cottage. They were tucking into toast and jam, and talking of all the things they had to do that day. It was going to be a very busy day indeed.

"I will need your help this morning Big Bamboo," said Pa. "We must plant some redcurrant bushes."

"And I have an extremely large batch of strawberry jam to make," said Grandma.

"I'm taking the twins into town to do some shopping," said Ma.

"Jam, jam, jam!" said baby Jim Jam.

"Oh dear," said Ma, looking worried. "Who is going to look after little Jim Jam? We are all too busy!"

"I have an idea," said Pa.
"The marmalade cat can look after him!"
And so it was decided that Jim Jam would
spend the day at the farm where his best
friend the marmalade cat lived.
Jim Jam was very excited.
The marmalade cat often came to
visit him at Tumbledown Cottage,
and had told him lots of things about the
farm and all the animals that lived there,
but Jim Jam had never been to visit.

Pa took Jim Jam to the farm in his big truck, and the marmalade cat met them at the gate. "Take good care of him," said Pa gruffly to the marmalade cat, as he waved goodbye. "And don't get into mischief, Jim Jam!"

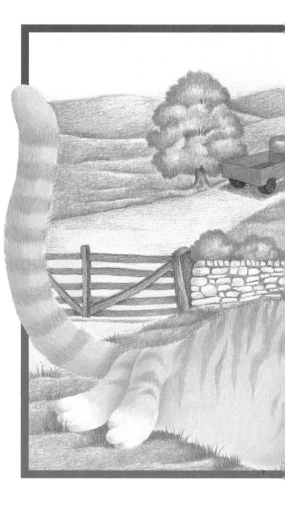

First, the two friends headed into the field full of sheep and little lambs. Jim Jam had never seen lambs before, and he was very excited. He crawled over to take a closer look. Mummy sheep looked up and gave a loud "Baaa!" as Jim Jam approached. She looked rather fierce and Jim Jam felt frightened. He turned and crawled away as fast as he could.

"Don't worry," said the marmalade cat, laughing at Jim Jam's scared face. "She won't hurt you. She is just taking care of her babies."

They carried on towards the duck pond.
"Let's go and see the ducks," said the
marmalade cat. But as Jim Jam was kneeling
down at the edge of the pond, taking a closer
look at the fluffy ducklings, mummy duck came
up behind him and gave a loud "Quack!" He
was so surprised that he fell into the pond with a
SPLASH! The marmalade cat soon fished him
out, but he was very wet. Poor Jim Jam!

Next, Jim Jam and the marmalade cat went
to visit the pigs in the pigpen. Jim Jam
wanted to make friends with the piglets, and
before the marmalade cat could stop him,
he had crawled under the gate, and onto the
back of the biggest piglet.

The piglet squealed in alarm, and ran
around the pigpen as fast as he could, trying
to shake Jim Jam off. "Wheee!" called Jim
Jam, before landing BUMP! in a pile of hay.

"Come along," said the marmalade cat. "Let's go and watch the cows being milked in the cowshed. They are much too big for you to ride on. You won't get into trouble there."

But this time it was little Jim Jam who frightened the big cow. She had never seen a panda before. With a loud "moo!" she kicked over the bucket of milk and it splashed all over Jim Jam.

"Oh dear," said the marmalade cat. "You are having a messy day Jim Jam!"

Last of all, they went to the hen house, where all the hens were busy laying eggs. Jim Jam liked the hens and the funny clucking sound they made and he was having a lovely time playing with the fluffy yellow chicks, when all of a sudden one of the hens gave a loud squawk and jumped up, knocking some eggs off the shelf. The eggs fell and broke on Jim Jam's head! A big fox was peering through the open door.

Little Jim Jam looked up and saw the fox. Inquisitive as ever, he decided to take a closer look, so he crawled across the hen house towards him. The fox took one look at Jim

Jam, turned on his tail and ran into the distance. The hens squawked with delight. Jim Jam had saved them!

"You really are quite a sight Jim Jam," laughed the marmalade cat. "No wonder you frightened the fox away!"

Back at the farm house, the marmalade cat soon cleaned Jim Jam up, and then he made sure that Jim Jam had a jammy tea to remember, with his favourite blueberry jam. All of Jim Jam's new friends from the farmyard crowded round him, and it turned into quite a celebration.

Just then Pa Jam arrived to take Jim Jam home.

"Have you been good?" asked Pa, sternly.

"He's been just *purrfect*!" said the marmalade cat, with a wink!

• T H E   E N D •